For dreamers everywhere —R.L.S.
For Susie —D.S.

First published in the United Kingdom in 2003 by
The Chicken House, 2 Palmer Street, Frome, Somerset, BA11 1DS
Email: *chickenhouse@doublecluck.com*

Library of Congress Cataloging-in-Publication data available
Reinforced Binding for Library Use

ISBN 0-439-53168-3

10 9 8 7 6 5 4 3 2 1 03 04 05 06 07

Printed in Singapore
First American edition, October 2003

The Sheep Fairy

When Wishes Have Wings

By
Ruth Louise Symes

Illustrated by
David Sim

The Chicken House
SCHOLASTIC INC.
New York

This is Wendy Woolcoat. Wendy likes:

eating grass
eating grass
eating grass
eating grass
eating grass
eating grass
eating grass
eating grass
eating grass
eating grass
sleeping
eating grass
eating grass
eating grass
eating grass
eating grass

One day Wendy was eating grass,
when a tiny voice said,

"Help me!
Please, help me."

It was a fairy, stuck in a brambly bush!

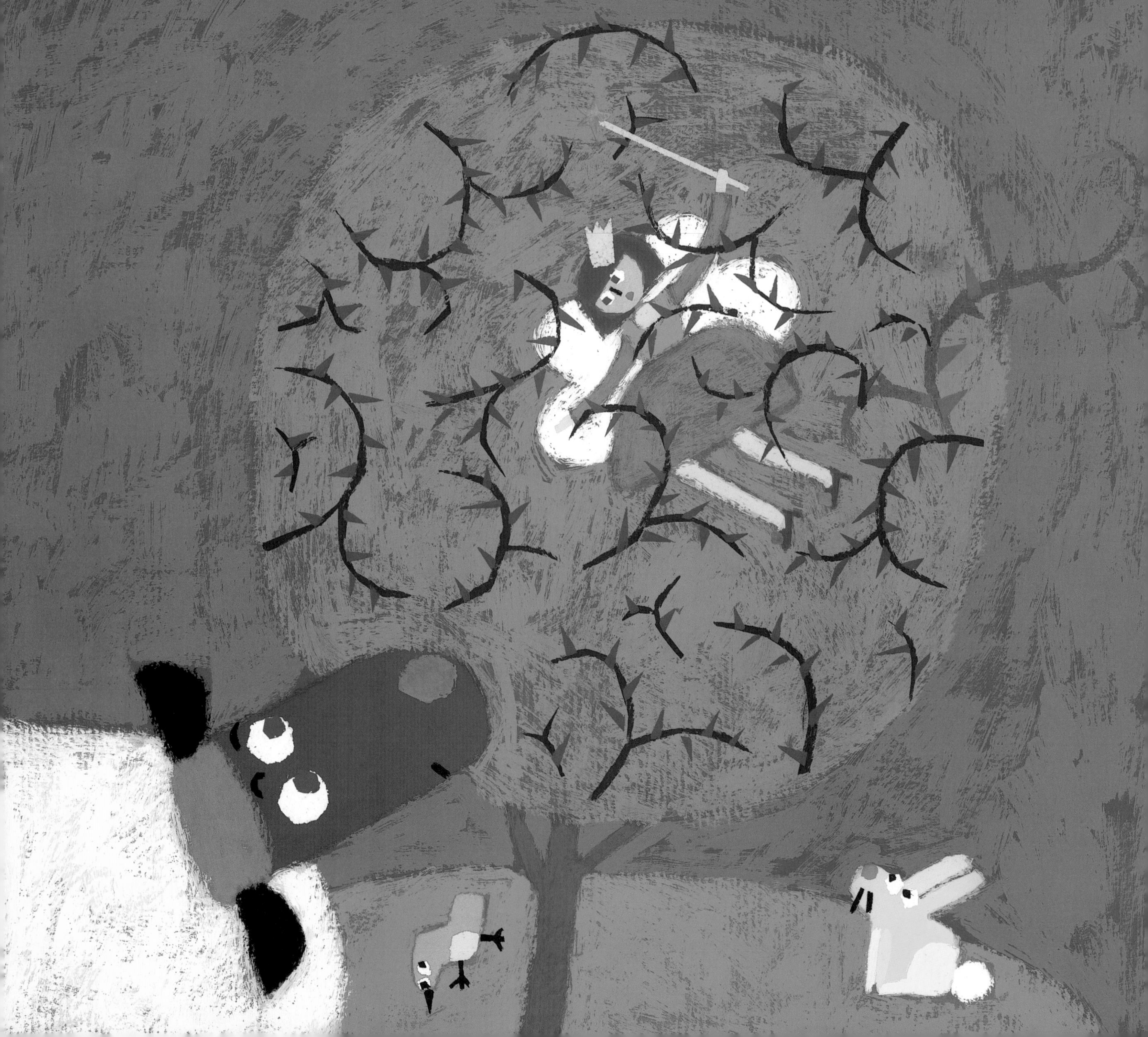

Wendy was a kind sort of sheep, so she ate all of the brambles around the fairy and set her free.

"Oh, thank you," said the fairy.
"As a special reward
for helping me,
I'll give you one wish.
What would you like?"

"Well," said Wendy, thinking hard.
"Mostly, I like eating grass
and sleeping."

"But you can do both of those already," said the fairy. "There must be something else you dream about."

"Oh, yes!" said Wendy. She'd never told anyone about her secret dream before, but very quietly she told the fairy.

"Speak up!" the fairy said. "I can't hear you."

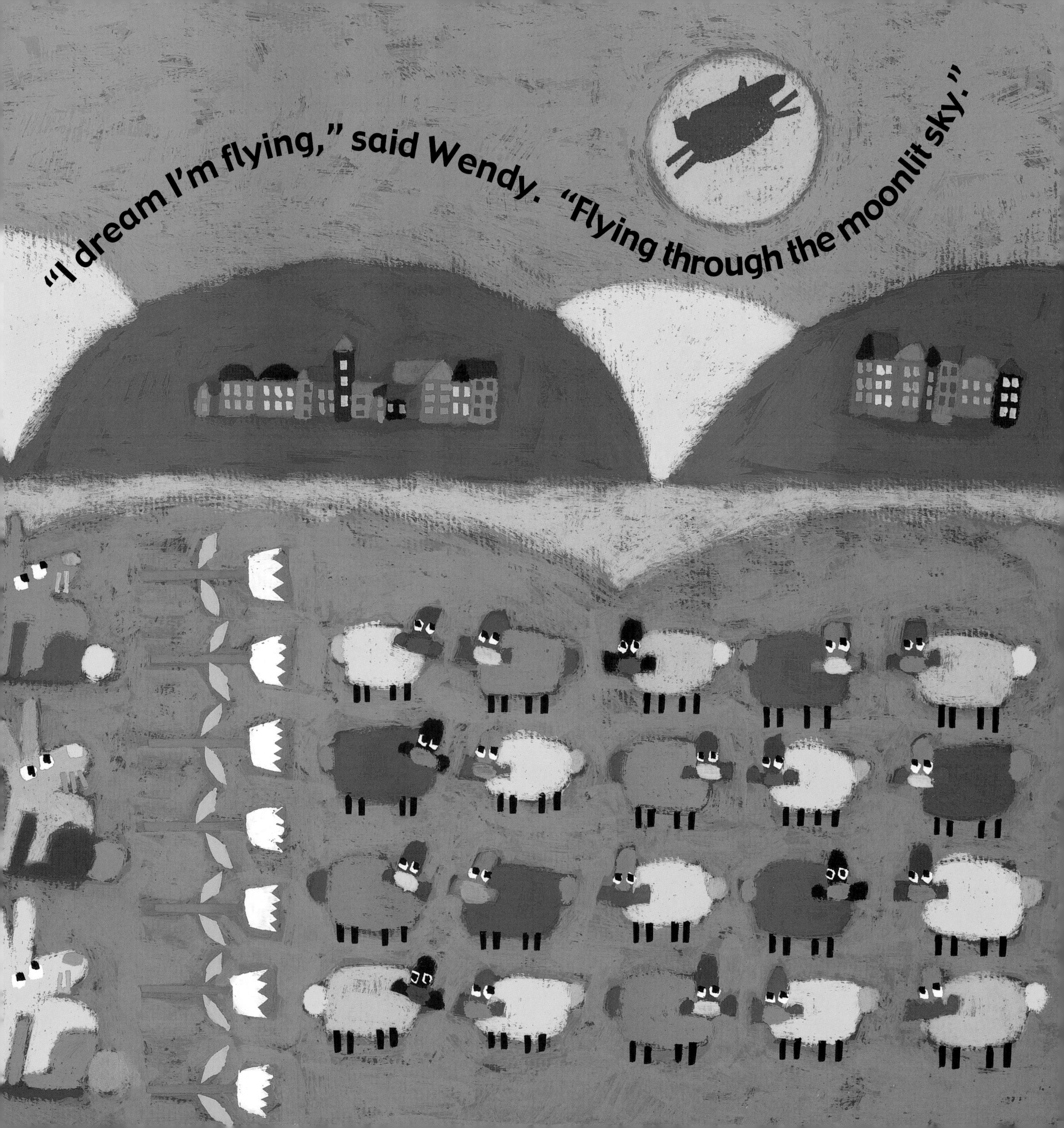
"I dream I'm flying," said Wendy. "Flying through the moonlit sky."

Wendy looked around quickly to see if any of the other sheep had heard her. They all had their heads down, eating grass. Wendy started to eat grass, too. It was delicious.

"When the moon comes up and the stars come out, your wish will come true," said the fairy as she flew off.

Wendy was much too busy eating grass to listen.

When the moon came up and the stars came out,
Wendy had a very strange feeling indeed.

She
felt
like
she
was
floating
upward.

The field was far below.

Wendy had grown
a pair of beautiful,
sheep-sized fairy wings
on her back. She flapped
them up and down.

"Baa," Wendy bleated
to the other sheep.
Then she wiggled
her legs around as though
she were running in the sky.

"Baa baa baa,
look at me —
I'm flying!"
But the other sheep
were fast asleep.

Soon she got the
hang of flying:

forward

backward

upward

downward

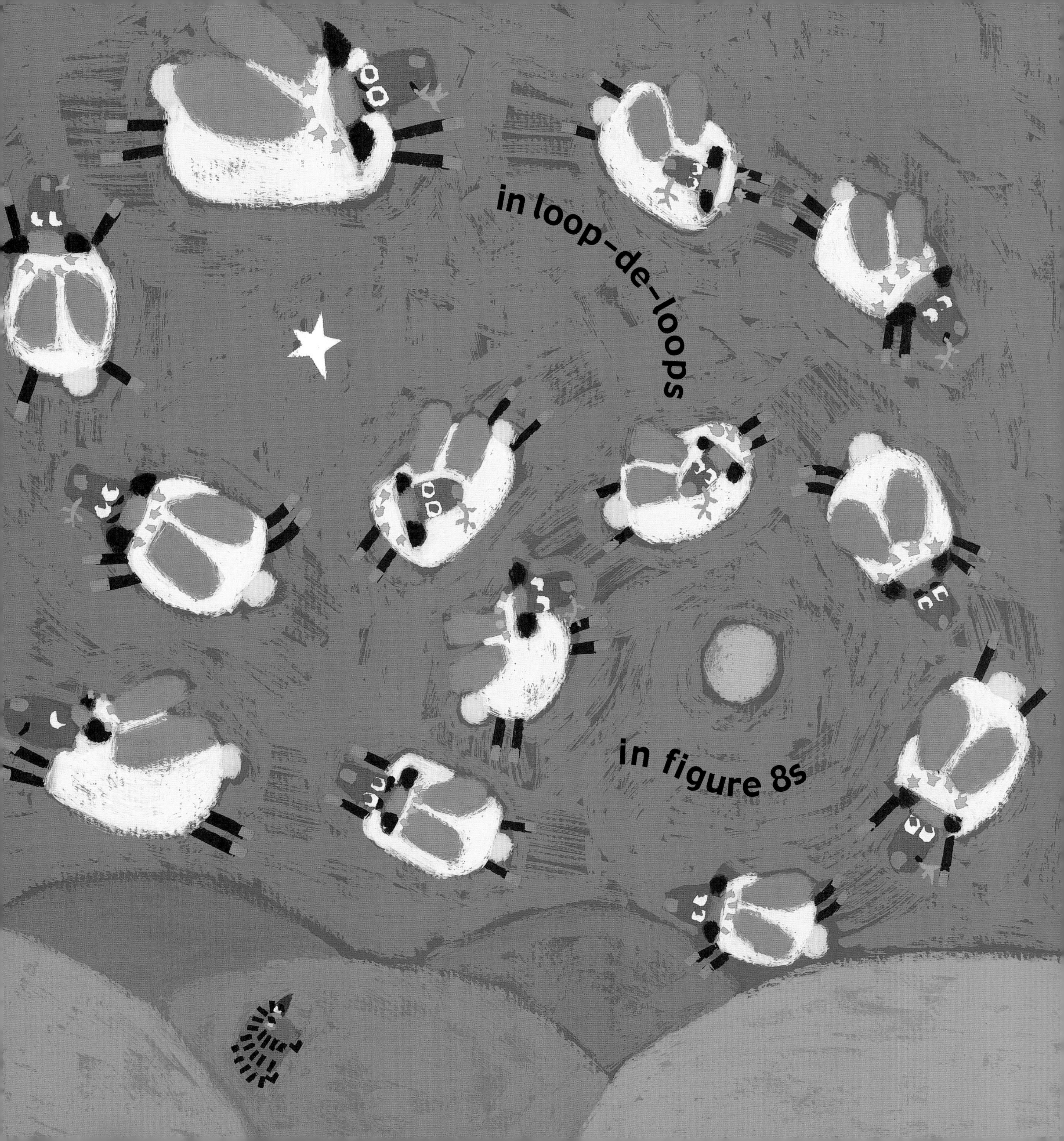
in loop-de-loops
in figure 8s

**Wendy flew
over the farmer's house
and through the town
and out to sea.**

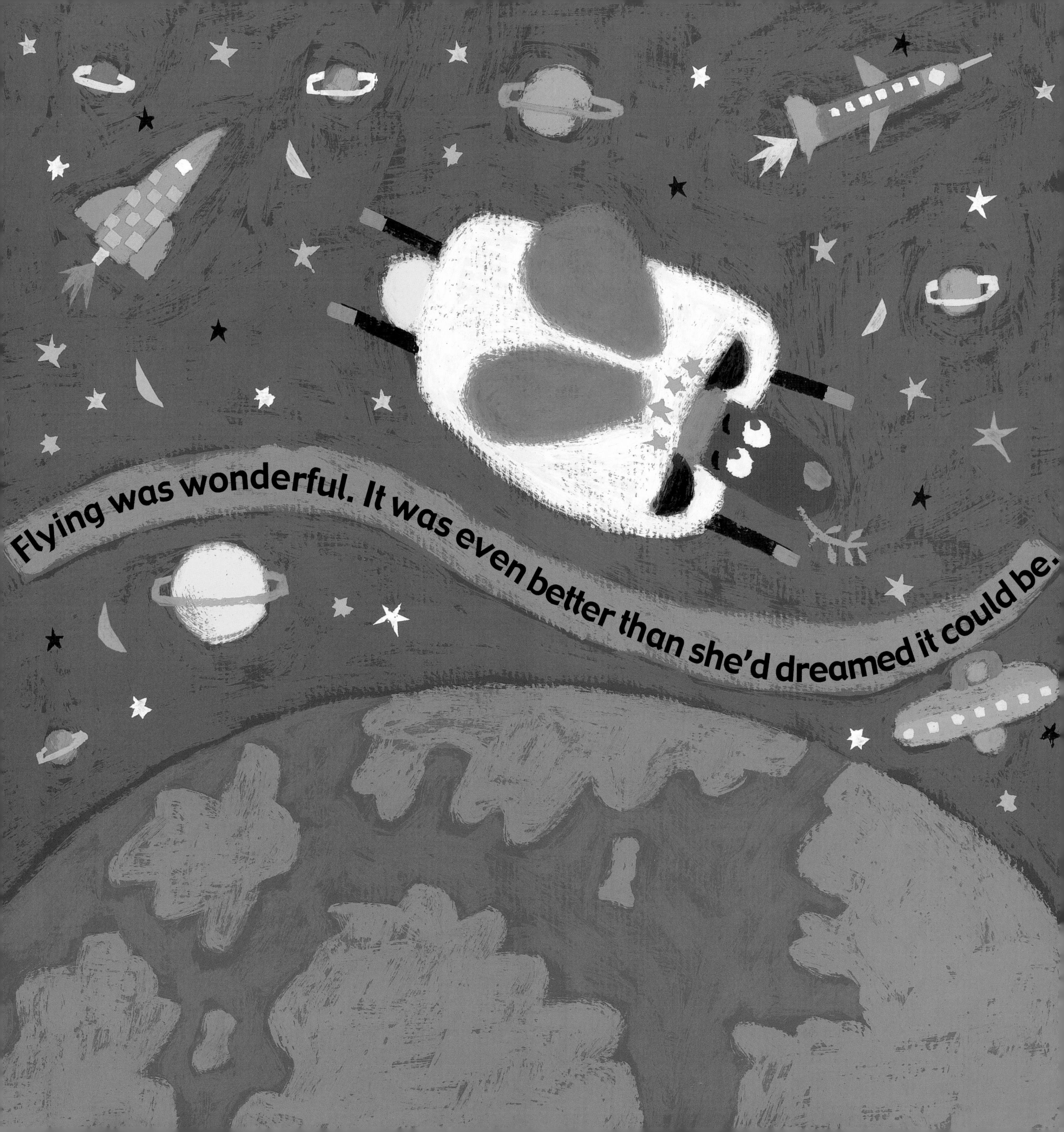

Flying was wonderful. It was even better than she'd dreamed it could be.

On the way back, Wendy saw a wolf strolling down the lane toward the sheep's field.

"Wake up, wake up! There's a wolf coming!" Wendy cried. But the sheep kept on sleeping. "Wake up, wake up. There's a wolf coming — and he's coming to get you!"

But the sheep still didn't wake up, and it was almost too late. The wolf was in the sheep's field. Wendy had to do something!

Wendy flew
straight at the wolf.
"Leave my friends alone
she shouted.

Help, Mommy!

The next morning
the sheep in Wendy's field were doing
what they did every morning:

eating grass

eating grass

eating grass

eating grass

"I had a really strange dream last night," said Sheep 1.

"Me, too," said Sheep 2.
"Me, three," said Sheep 3.

And all the other sheep agreed. "Baa baa baaa."

"I dreamed that Wendy could fly."

"That's what I dreamed."

"Me, too."
"Us, too."

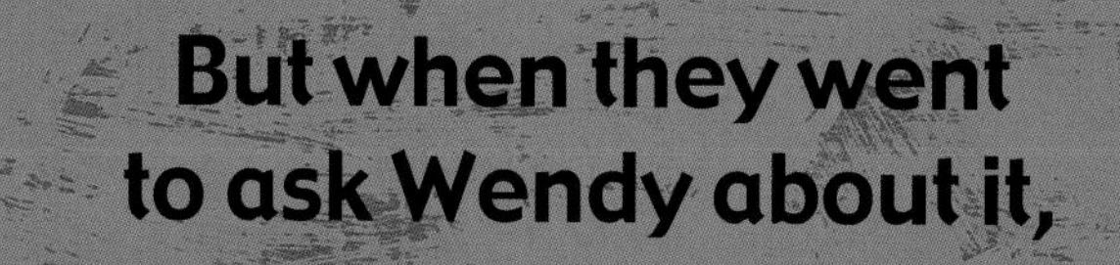

But when they went
to ask Wendy about it,

she was fast asleep.